Henny Penny

H. Werner Zimmermann

North Winds Press

A Division of Scholastic-TAB Publications Ltd.

Illustrations copyright © 1989 by H. Werner Zimmermann.
Text copyright © 1989 by Scholastic-TAB Publications Ltd.
All rights reserved.

98765432

Printed in Hong Kong

Canadian Cataloguing in Publication Data

[Chicken Licken]
   Henny Penny

Issued also in French under title: Picorine la poule.
ISBN 0-590-73159-9

I. Zimmermann, H. Werner (Heinz Werner),
1951-   II. Title.

PZ8.1.C43He 1989   398.24   C88-094303-3

To Kathryn Cole,
who keeps the sky from falling.

One day Henny Penny
was eating corn in the farmyard
when . . . .

whack! . . . an acorn fell on her head.

"Oh, my," said Henny Penny.

"The sky is falling! The sky is falling.
I must go and tell the King."

So she went along and she went along
and she went along until she met
Cocky Locky.

4

"Hello, Henny Penny," said Cocky Locky.
"Where are you going?"

"The sky is falling and I must go
and tell the King," said Henny Penny.

"Oh! May I go with you?" asked Cocky Locky.

"Certainly!" said Henny Penny.

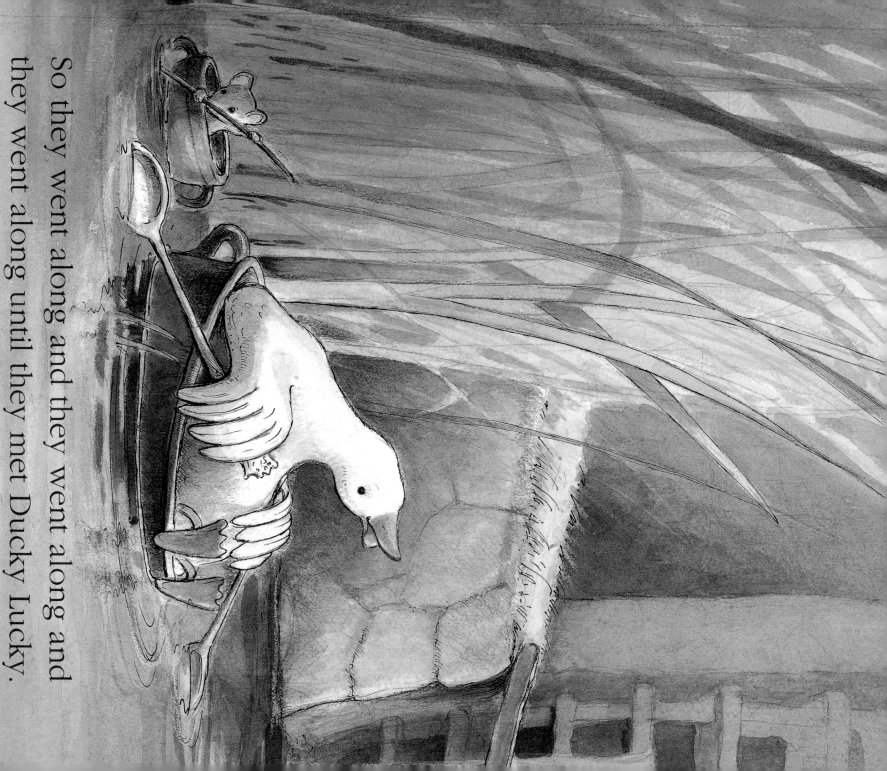

So they went along and they went along and they went along until they met Ducky Lucky.

8

"Hello, Henny Penny and Cocky Locky,"
said Ducky Lucky. "Where are you going?"

9

"The sky is falling and
we must go and tell the King,"
said Henny Penny and Cocky Locky.

10

"Oh! May I go with you?" asked Ducky Lucky.

"Certainly!" said Henny Penny and Cocky Locky.

So they went along and they went along and they went along until they met Goosey Loosey.

"Hello, Henny Penny, Cocky Locky and Ducky Lucky," said Goosey Loosey. "Where are you going?"

12

"The sky is falling and we must go and tell the King," said Henny Penny, Cocky Locky and Ducky Lucky.

"Oh! May I go with you?" asked Goosey Loosey.

"Certainly!" said Henny Penny, Cocky Locky and Ducky Lucky.

So they went along and they went along and
they went along and they went along until they met Turkey Lurkey.

14

"Hello, Henny Penny, Cocky Locky, Ducky Lucky and Goosey Loosey," said Turkey Lurkey. "Where are you going?"

"The sky is falling and we must go and tell the King," said Henny Penny, Cocky Locky, Ducky Lucky and Goosey Loosey.

"Oh! May I go with you?" asked Turkey Lurkey.

"Certainly!" said Henny Penny, Cocky Locky, Ducky Lucky and Goosey Loosey.

17

So they went along and they went along

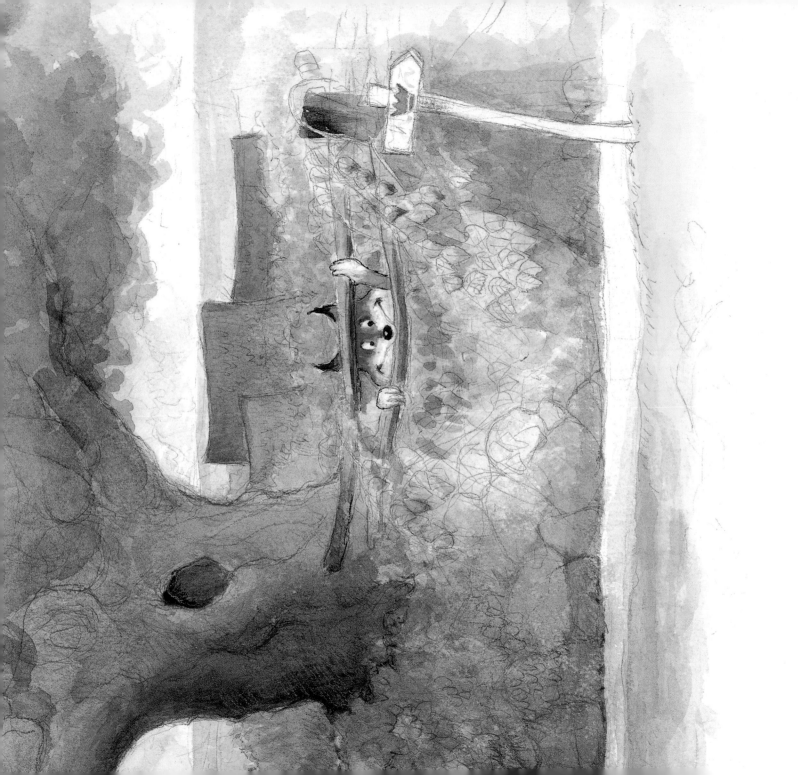

and they went along until until they met Foxy Loxy.

"Greetings, Henny Penny, Cocky Locky, Ducky Lucky, Goosey Loosey and Turkey Lurkey," said Foxy Loxy. "Where are you going?"

21

"The sky is falling and we must go and tell the King," said Henny Penny, Cocky Locky, Ducky Lucky, Goosey Loosey and Turkey Lurkey.

22

"You'll never get there in time," said Foxy Loxy. "Come with me and I'll show you the shortcut."

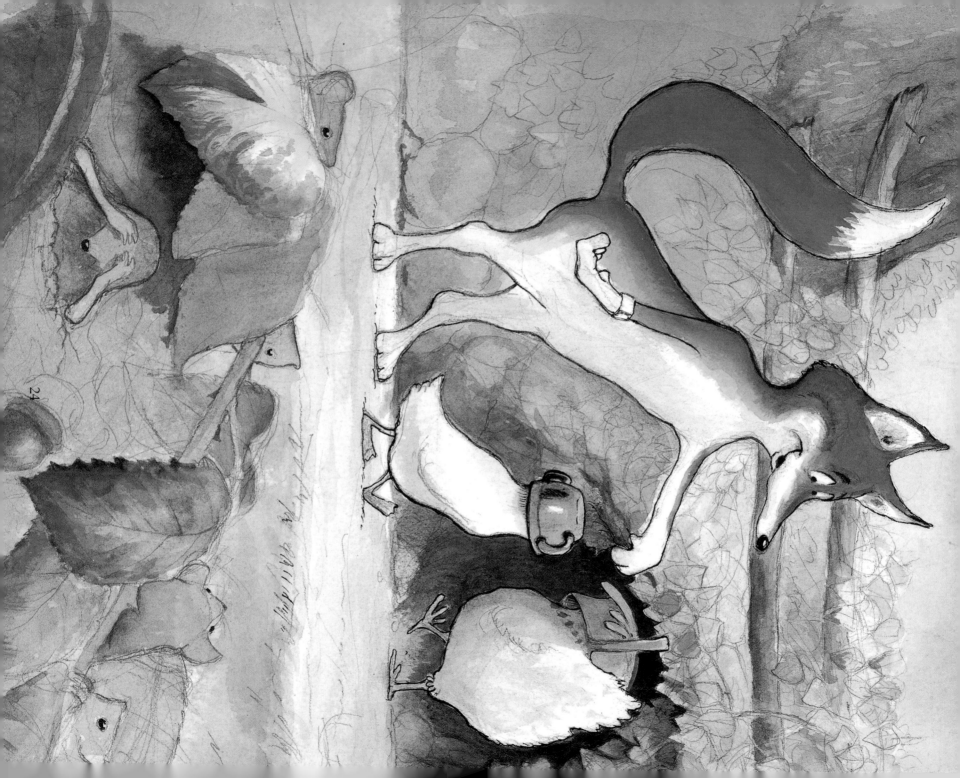

"Certainly!" said Henny Penny,
Cocky Locky, Ducky Lucky,
Goosey Loosey and Turkey Lurkey.
And they followed Foxy Loxy
right into his cave.

Henny Penny, Cocky Locky, Ducky Lucky,
Goosey Loosey and Turkey Lurkey were
never seen again . . .

. . . and no one ever told the King
the sky was falling.